KU-266-501

First published 2013 by Nosy Crow Ltd
The Crow's Nest, 10a Lant Street
London SE1 1QR
www.nosycrow.com

ISBN 978 0 85763 364 4

Nosy Crow and associated logos are trademarks
and/or registered trademarks of Nosy Crow Ltd.
John Lewis and associated logos are trademarks
and/or registered trademarks of John Lewis plc.

Text and Book Design Copyright © Nosy Crow Ltd 2013 licensed to John Lewis plc
Images and Concept Copyright © John Lewis plc 2013
All rights reserved

This book is sold subject to the condition that it shall not,
by way of trade or otherwise, be lent, hired out or otherwise circulated in
any form of binding or cover other than that which it is published.
No part of this publication may be copied, reproduced, stored in a retrieval system,
or transmitted in any form or by any means (electronic, mechanical, photocopying,
recording or otherwise), in whole or in part,
without the prior written permission of Nosy Crow Ltd and John Lewis plc.

A CIP catalogue record for this book is available from the British Library.

Printed in Italy
Papers used by Nosy Crow are made from wood grown
in sustainable forests.

3 5 7 9 8 6 4 2

The Bear
who had never seen
Christmas

 nosy crow

Bear and Hare were best of friends.
They both lived in the wood.
They walked and talked and played and sang —
the way that best friends should.

But, one day, when the wind blew cold,
Bear stopped and sniffed the air.
"The snow is on its way," he said.
"The winter's coming, Hare."

Hare sighed. He knew what winter meant —
his friend would sleep till spring.
And, curled up in a cave,
he'd miss the joy that Christmas brings.

For Christmas was a special time
that Bear would never see.
No fun, no games, no joy to share,
no singing round the tree.

"Oh, Bear," said Hare. "Why must you go?
Whatever will I do?
This Christmas, can't you stay awake,
and see the winter through?"

Bear looked at Hare and gently smiled.
"I wish I could," he said.
"But when it snows and chill winds blow,
a bear must be in bed."

Just as he spoke, a snowflake fell,
and landed on his nose.
"It's time to sleep," Bear sighed. "The year
is drawing to a close."

Bear looked sad and quite forlorn.
He didn't want to go.
"But what is Christmas like?" he said.
"I really want to know."

"Oh, Christmas is just wonderful!"
said Hare. "The woods are white,
and frost and sparkle fill the air,
and stars light up the night.

"Christmas looks just beautiful,
with glittering snow and ice.
And Christmas smells delicious,
with berries, herbs and spice.

"Christmas is a feeling.
It's a time for friends to share.
It's a time to come together,
every creature,
bird and . . .

. . . Bear?"

Bear had stopped to sit and rest.
He yawned and rubbed his eyes.
"I'm sleepy, I can't stay awake.
I'm sorry, Hare," Bear sighed.

With that, Bear slowly turned and left.
He walked off all alone.
He headed for the mountains,
and the cave, his winter home.

Hare watched Bear as he left a trail
of footprints in the snow.
His ears fell flat, his heart felt sad.
Why did Bear have to go?

Bear travelled over hills and lakes,
through woods and over streams,
and, as night fell, he found his cave,
his place to sleep and dream.

Hare thought and thought while Bear slept on.
"I need a plan," he said.
"Ah! I know just what I can do
to get him out of bed."

So, late one night, as midnight struck,
Hare set off at a run,
to make a Christmas dream come true
before the night was done.

Then with a parcel in his mouth,
he reached his best friend's lair,
and gently laid the parcel down —
his **special** gift for Bear.

Next morning, it was Christmas Day.
The sun shone bright and clear,
and all the creatures gathered round,
each full of love and cheer.

But Hare just watched and waited.
The snow-white hills were bare.
He hoped and hoped his friend would come,
but there was no-one there.

Hare heard a sound and turned again.
Whoever could it be?
"Could it be my best friend, Bear?
Can he see the Christmas tree?"

"It's Bear! It's Bear!" Hare shouted out.
"I'm so glad that you're here.
Now my Christmas is complete."
He smiled from ear to ear.

"You're just in time! I've such a lot
to show you and to share."
And sleepy Bear began to grin,
as Christmas filled the air.

But wait! What was the special gift
that woke Bear just in time?

A shiny new alarm clock
with bells that ring and chime!

The two friends gazed together
at the sparkling Christmas tree.
Hare gave a happy sigh,
Bear turned,
and said, contentedly . . .

"This is the Christmas feeling
that you wanted me to share —
a Christmas that I won't forget.
Oh, thank you,
thank you, Hare!"